The Tree Within The Tree

Sally Huss

ISBN 10:1945742062
ISBN 13: 9781945742064

It was the day before Christmas and the tree lay on a pile of discarded pine boughs.

A few other trees stood on the lot beckoning to the last-minute shoppers, "Take me! Take me!"

But, the tree knew that no one would take him. He was a scrawny, scraggly, undernourished tree with more than a few broken branches.

Then, two children came on the lot. The tree watched as they wandered through the few remaining trees, looking at the price tags on each and shaking their heads.

The lot man came over to them. "What can I do for you?" he asked.

"We would like a Christmas tree, but we only have two dollars."

"Ho! Ho! Ho!" laughed the lot man. "That won't buy a proper Christmas tree. But, you can have anything you can find in that pile over there for two dollars."

The children ran toward the heap of pine rubbish. The tree lay on top. They couldn't believe their eyes and the tree couldn't believe his eyes. "It's perfect!" they squealed, as they set him up and danced about.

The tree rose to the occasion and fluffed himself out as best he could – even that wasn't much.

Then, they grabbed him by his feet and headed for home.
"Thanks, Mister," they called to the lot man, who was beginning to
look a lot like Santa.

"Ho! Ho! Ho! Merry Christmas!" he yelled back at them, stuffing the two dollars into his pocket.

The tree couldn't believe his good fortune. He was going to be a Christmas tree after all.

Dragging the tree behind them, Alexander and Charlotte opened the door to their little home and called, "Mama! Mama! Charlie! Olivia! Lily!"

Mama and the younger children came running to see what all the fuss was.

Charlotte and Alexander brought their prize inside and stood

the tree up.

"Oh my, oh my," the sisters and brother exclaimed, as they

admired the tree. "It's beautiful. It's lovely. It's divine!" they agreed.

The tree was beside himself with all the attention. He was no longer the puny, withered excuse for a tree. With their praise, he became The Tree Within The Tree, a magnificent, full-bodied, full-scented, full-fledged Christmas tree!

"I know what we'll do," said Mama, clapping her hands together. "We'll decorate it."

"With what?" the children wanted to know.

"Anything and everything," said Mama, heading for the kitchen to pop some corn. The girls went to their room to see what they could find. The boys went to their room to do the same.

The tree was left alone. Look at me, he thought. I am The Tree Within The Tree. I am beautiful and that's the tree they see.

Then, he looked around the room. The chairs had chips on them. The curtains had stains. The couch had tears and the rug had spots. But, the room was beautiful to him because he loved it. It was his new home.

As he looked more closely, he began to see The Chairs Within The Chairs, The Curtains Within The Curtains, The Couch Within The Couch, and The Rug Within The Rug. And as he did, they all brightened because he loved them.

When everyone came back into the room, they brought their treasures.

Mama had a bowl of popcorn. With a needle and thread, she began stringing popcorn into garlands.

Charlie had found some tin foil and began making Christmas balls.

Olivia offered her ballerina doll with butterfly wings to sit on top of the tree.

Charlotte began tying her hair ribbons into Christmas bows.

Lily had collected several colorful baby rattles she wanted to hang on the branches.

And, Alexander found a pair of scissors, paper, markers, and glue. Surely something could be made with these, he thought.

The Tree Within The Tree stood proudly watching the activities of his new family.

Then, the fun began.

A ballerina angel was placed on his head.

Strings of popcorn swirled around his shoulders and arms.

Was it popcorn or were they pearls?

Tin ornaments hung from his wrists and elbows. Were they made of tin or was it silver?

A rattle here and there sounded joyful. Might they really be toy drums?

Strands of ribbons, turned into bows, could easily be mistaken for colorful doves.

And, small masterpieces made by small hands sat proudly on branches in just the right spots.

"No greater tree has there ever been," said Mama with a sigh.

"I love it!" said Charlotte.

"I love it!" said Alexander.

"I love it!" said Charlie.

"I love it!" said Olivia.

"I love it!" said Lily.

And, The Tree Within The Tree knew it was true because they loved what they had, not what they didn't.

On this wonderful Christmas Eve, where presents were few, but gifts were plenty, the greatest gift of all was given to the tree – the gift of appreciation. He now loved what he was, not what he wasn't. And, what he was, was perfect – The Tree Within The Tree!

The end, but not the end of being appreciative.

At the end of this book you will find a Certificate of Merit that may be issued to any child who has earned it. This fine Certificate will easily fit into a 5"x7" frame, and happily suit any girl or boy who receives it!

You may view Sally's collection of children's books by going to www.sallyhuss.com, where you may also sign-up to receive a free e-book and information regarding her free promotions. All books are available as e-books and as paperbacks. Here are just a few.

About the Author/Illustrator

"Bright and happy," "light and whimsical" have been the catch phrases attached to the writings and art of Sally Huss for over 30 years. Sweet images dance across all of Sally's creations, whether in the form of children's books, paintings, wallpaper, ceramics, baby bibs, purses, clothing, or her King Features syndicated newspaper panel "Happy Musings."

Sally creates children's books to uplift the lives of children and hopes you will join her in this effort by helping spread her happy messages.

Sally is a graduate of USC with a degree in Fine Art and through the years has had 26 of her own licensed art galleries throughout the world.

This certificate may be cut out, framed, and presented to any child who has earned it.

Certificate of Merit

_____
(Name)

The child named above is awarded this Certificate of Merit for:

*Appreciating others

*Appreciating the help others give you

*Appreciating yourself

Date: _____

Presented by: _____

Made in the USA
San Bernardino, CA
11 December 2018